OLD DOG, NEW TRICKS

The Story of an Old Shelter Dog Who Got a Second Chance

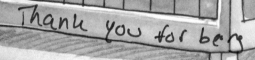

Thank you for being kind to animals ♥

Love,
Maribel
Vera
☺

Marie-Yolaine Williams

Illustrated by Richa Kinra

Old Dog, New Tricks
The Story of an Old Shelter Dog Who Got a Second Chance
All Rights Reserved.
Copyright © 2016 Marie-Yolaine Williams
v2.0

Illstrations by: Richa Kinra.
Illustrations © 2016 Outskirts Press, Inc. All rights reserved - used with permission.

http://www.outskirtspress.com

Paperback ISBN: 978-1-4787-6163-1
Hardback ISBN: 978-1-4787-6337-6

Outskirts Press and the "OP" logo are trademarks belonging to Outskirts Press, Inc.

PRINTED IN THE UNITED STATES OF AMERICA

DENVER, COLORADO

For old shelter dogs everywhere.
And for Langston, who sees their value.

Once there was a man named Mr. Pickett. He lived in a cozy little house on a quiet street in a very small town. Mr. Pickett was a very nice fellow. And he was old. One hundred and one years old to be exact. Mr. Pickett never married and had no children. Most of his friends had gone, but he had a dog named Boscoe who he adored. Boscoe was eleven years old.

Dogs age faster than humans. For every year a human lives, a dog lives seven years. This concept is called dog years. Boscoe was eleven, but in dog years, that is seventy-seven years old. If you put that in a math equation, it would look like this: 11 X 7 = 77.

During their time together, Mr. Pickett and Boscoe went on lots of walks. They also curled up on the sofa and watched old movies. On Saturdays, they got a special treat: vanilla frozen yogurt, which Boscoe loved. But Boscoe's favorite thing to do was sit and listen to Mr. Pickett read the newspaper. Boscoe sat attentively at Mr. Pickett's feet, hearing all about what was going on in the world. Every now and again, Mr. Pickett would stop reading, look at Boscoe, and say: "Well, I did not know that Boscoe! You learn something new every day." And Boscoe would wag his tail in agreement.

Then one day, Mr. Pickett felt very tired. He looked at Boscoe and said: "best buddy, I think it's my time to go." "I don't understand," Boscoe said, perplexed. "Where are you going?" Mr. Pickett smiled at him and replied: "I want you to know that, of all the souls I've met here on Earth, yours was by far the most loving, the most loyal, and the sweetest. You, Boscoe, are the greatest dog ever." Upon hearing this, Boscoe licked Mr. Pickett's hand. That night, Mr. Pickett died in his sleep. Boscoe was inconsolable.

A kind neighbor drove Boscoe to a nearby shelter after the funeral. "I wish I could keep you," she said, "but my little girl is allergic to dogs. I'm sure you will find a nice home. Don't worry. Everything will be fine."

At the shelter, Boscoe was panicked and scared. Some nice volunteers tried to make him feel better, but Boscoe missed Mr. Pickett. He missed having a bed, and he didn't like being in a cage most of the day. That first night at the shelter when the lights went out, Boscoe cried in his crate.

Every week on Saturdays, people came to the shelter to adopt dogs. A family came in one day and asked about Boscoe. "He's cute," the Dad said to a volunteer, "how old is he?" "He is eleven, and he's a great dog. He's housebroken and knows how to sit and stay. He gets along well with everyone." The volunteer went on: "his owner just passed, and he's quickly become a favorite around here." "You know the saying: 'you can't teach an old dog new tricks,'" the man said. "We're actually looking for a puppy," his wife chimed in.

Boscoe barked in protest. "What a silly saying! Mr. Pickett was old and he learned something new every day. We never stop learning, even when we get old." But the family moved on to look at puppies. And so it went every Saturday for five months. Boscoe was heartbroken. He used to love Saturdays, but now they made him so sad. "Everyone wants puppies," he lamented to himself, "I guess I'm here forever."

One Saturday, a family came in. They had an eight year old boy named Max. "We just lost our dog," Max's father explained, "he lived to be nineteen years old." "I'm so sorry to hear," a volunteer replied. "Thank you. We're looking for an older dog, one who is housebroken, good with children, and won't chew up Max's precious baseball card collection." Boscoe couldn't believe his ears! "Did they just say 'older dog?'" Boscoe wagged his tail in excitement. Max approached Boscoe's cage and pointed right at Boscoe. "I want this one Dad!"

Well, that Saturday ended up being one of the best Saturdays ever, because Boscoe got adopted! At his new home, he had a cozy bed, chew toys, stuffed animals, and a new best friend, Max. Max loved reading, which was great because Boscoe was already an expert at sitting attentively and listening. Only now, Boscoe wasn't hearing about current events. He was hearing stories about ninjas, wizards, dolphins, space, and other dogs. It was all so fascinating. "I had no idea ninjas were real," Boscoe thought to himself one day as Max was reading to him. "You really do learn something new every day." It got to the point where Max would pull out a book and Boscoe would wag his tail in anticipation. "Oh I hope it's the one about the wizards," he would think to himself, "I love that one." Max read to Boscoe so much that he became the best reader in his second grade class.

For seven years, Max and Boscoe enjoyed long walks, curling up on the sofa to read books, and eating vanilla frozen yogurt on occasion as a treat. Boscoe even learned a new trick: how to shake hands. When Boscoe learned this trick he was fourteen years old, which is ninety-eight years old in dog years. I guess you can teach an old dog new tricks after all!

Then, when Boscoe was eighteen, or as they say in dog years, one hundred and twenty six years old, he looked at Max, licked his hand, and said: "thank you for adopting me and for being my best friend. It's time for me to go be with my first owner, Mr. Pickett. You, Max, are the greatest big kid ever." That night, when Boscoe closed his eyes, the first thing he saw was his first owner, Mr. Pickett, running towards him. "There you are!" Mr. Pickett said, "I waited for you a long time!" Boscoe shook with delight and showered Mr. Pickett with kisses. And so Boscoe, the greatest dog ever, and his first owner, Mr. Pickett, watch lots of old movies, eat lots of vanilla frozen yogurt, and read a lot of newspapers.

But every now and again, Boscoe misses his friend Max, so he sneaks back down to Earth at night to give Max kisses while he sleeps. Whenever this happens, Max tells his parents at breakfast: "when I woke up, my ears and cheeks were wet. Boscoe must have paid me a visit last night to give me kisses in my sleep." "It's nice to see you still have that great imagination," his mother beams, while his father nods in agreement.

But Max knows the truth. So he eats his oatmeal and quietly gets ready for school, smiling to himself the entire time.

The End.

HOW YOU CAN HELP

Encourage your parents to adopt a dog or a cat from a shelter instead of going to a breeder or a pet store.

If your family decides to adopt a dog or a cat, won't you consider an older forever friend? They make wonderful companions!

If now is not the right time to adopt, ask your parents if you can foster an animal. Fosters provide temporary homes for pets while they wait to be adopted. Fostering saves lives!

If now is not the right time to have any pet in the house, there are other ways you can help. Consider sponsoring a dog or cat that is in a shelter. Shelters need money for food, vet services, and beds. You can raise some of the money needed by operating a lemonade stand, having a birthday fundraiser, or having a yard sale. This is a great way to help, even if your family can't commit to a dog at the moment.

Contact your local shelter and find out how you can help.

There are so many ways you can help dogs and cats who are homeless. Can you think of any others?

A percentage of the author's royalties will be donated to Susie's Senior Dogs, an organization that provides exposure to older dogs in shelters looking for their forever homes, as well as Lifeline Animal Project.

ABOUT THE AUTHOR'S SENIOR DOGS

FENSTER is a 10 year old Beagle mix who was adopted from Atlanta Pet Rescue when he was a puppy. He may be mixed with Corgi and Jack Russell. His favorite things are sleeping, playing with his friends, getting belly rubs, and all things food related. His favorite books are: "George Washington Carver," by Samuel and Beryl Epstein, and "Dog Heroes," by Mary Pope Osbourne. Fenster's favorite day is Halloween, and he loves Michael Jackson. His favorite CD is Mariah Carey's "Merry Christmas."

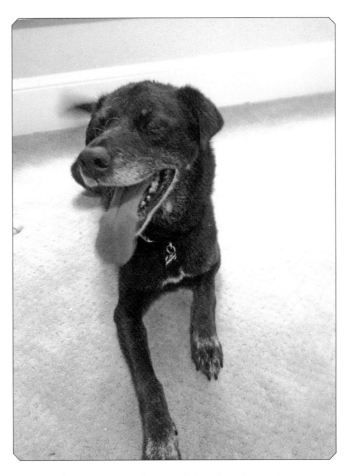

KEATON was adopted in June 2015 after she was picked up as a stray by Fulton County Animal Services. The vet estimates she is between 8 and 10 years old. She is a Black Lab. She loves to go for long walks and get belly rubs. Keaton also loves sleeping in her light up tepee. Her favorite books are: "Nubs, the True Story of a Mutt, a Marine, & a Miracle," by Major Brian Dennis, Kirby Larson, and Mary Nethery, and "Harry Potter and the Sorcerer's Stone," by JK Rowling. Her favorite CDs are Seth MacFarlane's "Music is Better Than Words" and "No One Ever Tells You."

CPSIA information can be obtained
at www.ICGtesting.com
Printed in the USA
LVIC06n1111310816
502645LV00003B/3